SERVICE LEARNING FOR TEENS™

PROTECTING THE ENVIRONMENT THROUGH SERVICE LEARNING

DON RAUF

ROSEN PUBLISHING®
New York

Published in 2015 by The Rosen Publishing Group, Inc.
29 East 21st Street, New York, NY 10010

First Edition

Library of Congress Cataloging-in-Publication Data

Rauf, Don.
Protecting the environment through service learning/Don Rauf.
pages cm.—(Service learning for teens)
Includes bibliographical references and index.
ISBN 978-1-4777-7961-3 (library bound)
1. Service learning—Juvenile literature. 2. Environmental protection—Juvenile literature. I. Title.
LC220.5.R38 2015
361.3'7—dc23

2014018166

Manufactured in the United States of America

CONTENTS

INTRODUCTION

Service learning is a type of education that is spreading across the country. Students in many high schools today are required to participate in service-learning projects in order to graduate. While it combines classroom instruction with community service, the emphasis of service learning is on the activities that students perform outside of the classroom to improve their community, school, and/or world. Through service learning, students nationwide may provide assistance at homeless shelters, build low-cost housing, tutor underprivileged children, and help with projects that improve the environment.

More students are participating in programs that help the environment and teach them about science and other subjects. Students in Maryland for example, have been active in a project called Bringing Back the Eastern Oyster.

According to the Corporation for National Service in a research project focused on environmental service learning, many young adults identify the environment as a main focus of concern.

In some environmentally oriented programs, young adults have donated their time, energy, and muscles to plant trees and bushes in local parks. They have cleaned up streams, rivers, and beaches where people have littered. They have organized campaigns to gather signatures in support of environmental efforts, such as banning plastic shopping bags, which are not biodegradable. Many of these students are passionate about this work and the learning experiences it provides because they realize that the Earth's resources are limited and are often threatened by pollution and other factors. They want to do what they can to contribute to a cleaner world where nature and living creatures can thrive.

Students who participate in service learning as part of a school requirement are typically asked to reflect on their community experience and think about how their service experience connects to their academics. Often, by writing out this reflection, they realize how their studies can be applied in a real-world setting.

Every student who attends a public school in Maryland participates in service learning as a part of their regular curriculum, and over 60 percent of these projects relate to the environment. Students from elementary, middle, and high schools in Calvert County participated in a project called Bringing Back the Eastern Oyster.

Oysters were once plentiful in the Chesapeake Bay, an estuary surrounded by Maryland and Virginia. In the late 1800s, more than fifteen million bushels of oysters were harvested from the waters of the Bay, but in current times, this number has dropped to under seventy-five thousand bushels. Overharvesting and declining water quality have led to the rapid disappearance of oysters. The oyster population in the Bay is said to currently be less than 1 percent of what it once was.

Through their participation in the Bringing Back the Eastern Oyster project, students helped scientists to create a new oyster habitat by releasing healthy oyster larvae onto designated oyster bars in the Patuxent River. Their experience with the ecology and restoration of the Chesapeake Bay's oyster reef connected to their science curriculum. Many of the participating students then went back to their schools and homes and taught friends and family about the importance of a healthy Chesapeake Bay. Some students also joined advocacy activities, making posters and writing letters to inform the community of this project.

Through hands-on activities with oysters, these students learned about the influence of water quality on the growth and survival of aquatic organisms, such as oysters. Students discovered the impact that disease and human activities can have on the natural world, and they also learned that damage to the environment can be reversed. These young adults made a difference in improving the environment while gaining firsthand experiences with scientific research.

Service learning can be a great motivator for many students. Not only does it provide the satisfaction of making the world a better place, but it also makes learning more fun and shows how learning in the classroom can be applied in the real world. These programs also give young people a sense of civic responsibility by asking students to look outside of themselves and help the common good.

This book will help students who are interested in this engaging way of learning to find out their options, to get involved, and to make the most of the service-learning experience.

CHAPTER ONE

GETTING YOUR HANDS DIRTY TO MAKE THE WORLD A BETTER PLACE

At the Milford Alternative Program in Connecticut, twenty-two high school students volunteered at the Milford Coastal Audubon, an organization dedicated to conserving Connecticut's environment through science-based education. The organization focuses on the state's bird populations and their habitats.

These students participated in Youth: Ethics in Service (YES), a service-learning experience led by their science teacher to help survey, plot, remove, and replace invasive plant species at the Audubon's nature sanctuary. As the students improved the grounds, they also learned about invasive species and their effects on the Connecticut coastline.

These students also worked in teams to restore more than five acres of Wilcox Park in Milford. They cleaned and rebuilt areas that had been damaged by bikers and hikers who had strayed from the existing trails.

Working with the City of Milford Tree Commission, these young people also planted trees at Walnut

Students involved in service learning are not afraid to get their hands dirty. Many work hard planting trees, cleaning parks, and mending trails. Students earn volunteer service hours while making the world a better place.

Beach, located on the Connecticut coastline. The students put in three days of hard labor. They dug holes and planted sourwood and serviceberry trees. These projects helped the city, the environment, and the students, who earned required volunteer service hours.

One student said: "This project is great because it really lets us learn. Usually I am really bored in class, but I have learned more in this one semester than I ever learned in my regular science classes."

LEARNING, LABORING, AND LOVING IT

Even though some service-learning opportunities require hard work and grueling hours, many students appreciate this type of learning experience more than learning in the classroom. By making a difference in the world, and actually doing rather than just reading and writing, students are able to gain a real sense of how their academics can be applied in the real world.

Students around the United States have made a positive impact on the environment in many different ways through service learning. In many schools, students must perform a minimum number of community service hours to graduate.

In Fairfax County Public Schools in Virginia, students must complete forty hours of service learning by the time they graduate, usually completing about ten hours a year from grades nine through twelve. In Seattle, Washington, schools, students must complete sixty hours of service learning in order to graduate.

At Ballard High School in Seattle, members of the Ballard Earth Service Corps have put time into neighborhood projects that are making a positive impact on the environment. For one event, the teens in the Earth Service Corps collected old and/or used bikes that people longer needed. They then donated the bicycles to Bike Works, an organization that repairs and gives the bikes to youth and adults in need of bikes. Getting more people to ride bikes is one way to cut down on air pollution, with the added benefit that individuals get more exercise. In fact, physical activity is one of the fringe benefits of most environmental service work.

The Ballard students have also cleaned up parks, started a school-wide composting program, and taught freshman classes about what materials can be composted and recycled. To encourage their fellow students

FIND SERVICE LEARNING THAT'S RIGHT FOR YOU

There are many options to choose from when it comes to service-learning opportunities. A school district or an individual school may offer a list or directory of programs to choose from, or students can come up with their own service-learning ideas. Students should think about their own interests. If you are scientifically oriented, you may want to work in a lab. For example, an organization may need help testing water samples for pollutants. If you enjoy writing, you may be able to put your writing skills to use by doing research, writing reports, and perhaps creating educational materials.

Think about the talents you have and which ones you'd most like to develop further. Be sure to talk to people who are involved in the programs that interest you. Group leaders and students can give you a real view of what a specific service-learning experience is like. Their tips and advice can be valuable in gaining the most from a program. Also, be aware of any possible deadlines to participate in a program and check to see if there is an application due date or any other requirements that must be met to join. To earn credit for service hours, students will most likely be asked to keep a log showing what type of work they have performed and the number of hours they have worked. An administrator or official with the volunteer project will sign a log sheet to verify the hours worked.

Sometimes, it takes just a few hours to make a positive impact on the environment. Students in Seattle removed invasive ivy and blackberries from a local beach in one afternoon.

to conserve, Earth Service Corps members suggested writing drafts on the backs of paper that already have printing or writing on one side. They also promoted biking to school, which conserves fuel by not using gas to drive.

Service-learning projects don't have to require a lot of time to make a difference. In one afternoon, Ballard students joined forces with students from another local high school and removed invasive blackberries and ivy at a local beach. They then planted new plants that are native to the area. Native plants are typically best suited to the conditions of a particular geographic region. Since native plants have taken centuries to adapt to the conditions, they are usually resistant to disease and pests, and they require less work and resources to maintain. Invasive plants can take over an area and take away from the natural diversity of an area that makes it thrive.

A WIDE WORLD OF OPPORTUNITIES

Youth Service America is a nationwide program dedicated to helping young people, ages five to twenty-five, get involved in community service. The program awards grants totaling more than one million dollars a year to youth, educators, and organizations to conduct service-learning programs.

The organization also offers ideas for service-learning programs for those who need inspiration or help getting started. Many of these programs are environmentally oriented. Examples include:

- Adopt a local park or green space near the school, and arrange with the park's management to plant and maintain a section of the park. Research how green spaces help a community, and develop an advertising campaign to promote the use of the park.
- Learn about the resources needed to manufacture athletic shoes and the amount of landfill space used to dispose of them. Create a campaign to recycle athletic shoes at your school.
- Study the impact of litter on marine plant and animal habitats. Team up with other youth to organize a beach cleanup day at a nearby beach. Sort

To earn school credit, some students "adopt" a park or green space. They plant vegetation and pick up litter (and recycle what they can) to improve the overall look of the land.

and quantify the litter retrieved, and present the findings at your school to encourage others not to litter our beaches.

- Buy local. Analyze the environmental impact of transporting goods and materials to different parts of the country and throughout the world. Research the goods and services produced in your region by visiting local businesses. Create a local print or electronic media campaign to explain the products and the benefits of shopping locally.
- Computer recycling. Learn about the kinds of materials used to build computers, and investigate how these materials can be either disposed of safely or recycled. See if you can partner with a local electronic-waste recycler, or create a brochure that explains to your community how to recycle unwanted electronics.
- Design a hydroelectric car. Research the history of automobile manufacturing in the United States and around the world. Learn about contemporary and alternative car designs and how each affects the environment and your community.
- Energy audits. Research the ways in which energy use affects the environment, and explore how individuals and organizations can reduce their energy consumption. Conduct an audit, or systematic analysis, in your school or at a community facility to determine if and how energy use can be reduced. Share the results of the audit with your school or organization.
- Garage sale. Organize a garage sale at your school for items that can be reused or recycled,

and be sure to spread the word at your school and community-focused outlets. Select a local nonprofit organization to receive proceeds from the sale.

- Green schools. Learn about ways to make your school green. Examine your school's initiatives in waste reduction, resource conservation, and energy use. Reach out to other schools and assist or advise them on greening their campuses.
- Local natural resource planning and management. Learn how cities, counties, and states manage natural-resources, and then investigate such resources in your own community. Design a resource-management plan that you can share with community members and local government officials.
- Make eco-friendly cleaners. Learn how the chemicals contained in traditional household cleaning items can affect humans and the environment. Research other methods of cleaning that are more environmentally friendly, and see if you can produce some for your school or local community agencies.
- Raise honeybees. Learn about the role of honeybees in the American food production industry and issues resulting from the declining bee population. Raise honey to share with local community organizations.
- Reduce school cafeteria waste. Apply what you learn in math and science classes to calculate how much food your school cafeteria throws away

There are many options when it comes to starting an environmental service-learning program. Raising bees is one possibility—students learn of the vital role bees play in nature and are rewarded with honey.

every day, and determine ways to reduce this waste. Share this information with your school board, and create strategies to reduce the waste and to implement food waste-reduction programs.

- Reduce energy consumption. Learn how various habits can affect each person's energy use and how these habits impact the environment. Create an "energy use" calendar or challenge your classmates, families, and other members of the community to reduce their consumption.

- Save water. Research and evaluate how your community uses water and how much it needs. Your local water bureau can provide information about how water can be conserved. Create a tip sheet with water-conservation strategies to distribute to parents and community members, and create a coloring book illustrating the tips for children.
- Sustainable building practices. Learn about which building materials and methods used in the United States and other countries have had a negative impact on the environment. Investigate alternative building methods and create a summary or brochure to share with local contractors or other community members.
- Trash audit. Investigate where trash in your community eventually ends up and its environmental impact. Analyze your school's trash, and determine how much of it can be reused or recycled. Share this data with your school to encourage more recycling on the premises.
- Vacant lot cleanup. Identify a vacant lot in the community that may need to be cleaned or beautified. Contact the lot's owner to secure permission to access and restore the property. Organize a cleanup event to remove both trash and invasive plant material from the lot.

CHAPTER TWO

HOW TO MAKE THE MOST OF A SERVICE-LEARNING OPPORTUNITY

According to a report from the Chicago Public Schools, nine out of ten high school students say that they learn best through hands-on learning, and that's exactly what service learning provides.

At Stephen T. Badin High School in Hamilton, Ohio, juniors and seniors can earn one credit for volunteer work donated to the community. Students spend two hours per week per semester in the field—a half-hour every Monday, Tuesday, Wednesday, and Thursday. The students also spend the first and last two weeks of the semester in the classroom, where they are trained for their upcoming service-learning experiences. On Fridays, students return to the classroom to hand in weekly journals and assignments and to discuss their experiences with classmates.

Earth Corps is a worldwide organization that promotes volunteering to help the environment. The group has individual clubs in many high schools around the country. At the Earth Corps club at Olympia High School in Olympia, Washington, students meet in the biology classroom at 8:15 AM on Wednesdays before first

Have you ever thought about where old cell phones go when they die? Electronics recycling programs reuse materials from the phones and prevent certain toxic components from entering the environment.

period and discuss their ideas for actions they can take together to help the environment in their community.

One of their successful campaigns was to organize a drive to collect used or outmoded cell phones for recycling. Cell phones contain precious metals, copper, and plastics. These metals are particularly valuable resources. Recycling conserves these elements and also curbs additional air and water pollution that results from the processes used to mine these metals. When old cell phones are incinerated or disposed of in landfills, the lead, mercury, cadmium, arsenic, and other flame-retardants they contain can contaminate the soil, ground water, and air.

Earth Corps student members realized that just holding a drive to collect cell phones may not be enough to inspire students to bring their old cell phones in, so they provided an incentive: home-baked cookies. Baked treats proved to be just the enticement needed to motivate students, and cell phones rapidly filled the collection boxes.

When the Earth Corps student members decided they wanted to make more of an impact locally, they reviewed issues that could have an effect on the city of Olympia. An item in the news caught their interest. With twenty-two acres, Little Baseball Association (LBA) Park is one of Olympia's largest green spaces, but an area connected to the park filled with trees and trails had come under threat by a housing developer. The City of Olympia was giving serious consideration to selling the property to the developer, but many who wanted to maintain this natural oasis opposed the development. The Earth Corps student members decided to take political action. They organized a petition and collected hundreds of signatures opposing building on this wilderness area, which provides a wildlife refuge in an urban setting. To promote the cause, the students created posters that showed how the development would impact nature in the area.

Students who volunteer their time with Earth Corps at Olympia High show how service-learning opportunities can build various skills that may help them throughout their lives. These students learned how to start a grassroots effort that could spur political change. They found out how to gather together the voices of many to make a difference in political decisions in their city. Their teamwork, promotion, and leadership influenced the course of events in their community and made them active members of their community.

SKILLS THAT CAN SERVE THROUGHOUT LIFE

In general, service learning offers experiences that students can use to build their résumés and help them throughout their careers. These skills are not only useful to open job doors—they are also useful in most employment opportunities. Here are some of the key skills that can be developed in almost any service-learning program and prove helpful in any work environment:

- **Time management.** Students have the opportunity to prove that they can show up on time and get their work done on schedule. A quote, often attributable to Woody Allen, is "90 percent of success is just showing up," and this really is important in the workplace. Employers value a worker who is dependable, shows up on time, and is ready to put in the hours required to get the work done. Another aspect of time management is being able to organize time to complete a task. Sometimes this requires breaking the task down into smaller components, and then scheduling exactly how and when to get the job done. Service learning often provides the experience of planning a big project and creating a schedule to finish tasks and complete an entire job.

- **Initiative.** Employers value a worker who will step up and take on work not asked of them. When students complete tasks that are asked of them, they can also step up and ask for additional work, or they can suggest ways to improve operations. This ability to take measures to make an operation more efficient is a plus on a résumé. For example, if you came up with a faster way to clean up trash in a park and dispose of the trash, this is an accomplishment worth noting.
- **Appearance.** Service learning is an opportunity to show that you can maintain a professional appearance. It may seem like common sense, but a worker who is clean and neatly dressed conveys a professionalism that employers trust. Group leaders of service-learning programs will note this among their students, and when it comes time to write recommendations, this may be an influencing factor.

Service-learning programs can offer valuable workplace skills that can help in a future career. Students often learn about time management, teamwork, leadership, communication, critical thinking, and more.

- **Behavior.** Students working in service learning have a chance to learn and demonstrate productive workplace attitudes and behavior. Service learning is an environment to show respect to others with a positive, "can-do" attitude and a friendly manner.
- **Communication skills.** Those who take on service learning need to be confident when expressing their ideas. They are often tasked with speaking before a group to explain their ideas or how to accomplish a project. While these experiences provide a means to practice verbal presentation, they may also offer a chance to refine written communication. A student may write a proposal or plan to explain exactly how a program's goals will be reached.
- **Critical thinking.** Service-learning projects tackle issues that require analysis and evaluation in order to form a judgment. This is a skill that goes hand and hand with problem solving.
- **Teamwork.** No matter what type of environmental service learning one chooses, teamwork is almost guaranteed to be a part of it. Students learn to collaborate to reach common goals. Knowing how to effectively interact with other students is a talent that comes only from experience, and service learning provides many opportunities to work together with others. Some environmental programs, such as cleanup efforts, introduce students who have never met each other before, and students have to quickly learn how to interact productively with others.

- **Leadership.** In addition to teamwork, service-learning projects also require leadership. Students make decisions on what course a program should take and who should do what to achieve goals (in other words, delegate). Good leaders are effective communicators, and they

SELF-QUIZ: WHAT DO YOU WANT FROM SERVICE LEARNING?

To better define what you'd like to gain from a service-learning experience, answer the questions below. Taking time for self-reflection and looking at expectations and personal goals can improve the service-learning experience.

- **What types of environmental issues would you like to explore?**
- **What experiences and skills do you hope to gain from this opportunity?**
- **Will you have a chance to lead, organize, and work with others? Is there an opportunity to take on a role as a coordinator?**
- **What skills and talents do you already bring to a volunteer project, and how can these skills and talents be used in the service-learning opportunity?**
- **How does this environmental service-learning experience apply to your academic and career goals?**

often have the ability to inspire others to join in and get the job done. They know how to stay calm when challenges arise. They are confident, committed, and positive. They are creative thinkers who come up with innovative ways to reach goals. And leaders sometimes have that intangible quality called intuition.

SPECIFIC CAREER-RELATED SKILLS

The talents and skills discussed so far can apply to any job, but some service-learning experiences provide training that may apply to specific "green" careers. A student involved in efforts to recycle and safely dispose of waste and discarded items might research the laws in his or her community or state that spell out how waste should be properly disposed of. For example, California has a website called CalRecycle that summarizes all the rules, codes, and laws pertaining to waste disposal and waste management. Students can find out the legal and proper way to dispose of hazardous materials, such as old paint, propane tanks from barbecue grills, and old fluorescent light bulbs.

These regulations touch upon environmental law, and students may get interested in this field from here. The Sierra Club, an environmental group dedicated to protecting the wild places of the Earth, says that environmental lawyers focus on laws concerning a wide range of issues including air and water quality, wildlife protection, and resource management. Environmental lawyers develop policies and engage in lawsuits to prevent environmental damage, compel waste cleanup, tighten regulations, or compensate individuals for harm due to environmental contamination.

Students interested in a career in science may find service-learning opportunities in which they help to analyze water samples for pollutants or research the exact toxic elements in discarded cell phones, computers, and

Some environmental programs give students the opportunity to get hands-on training for a future career. Students may be able to work in scientific research labs, for example, analyzing and cataloging samples.

other electronic devices. They may be involved with a program to capture and conserve rainwater. Each of these fields requires engineering and scientific know-how. In their pursuit of environmental learning, a student may discover issues directly related to the ways that chemical and biological elements can harm the human body. Environmental health is a field that addresses concerns that can hurt otherwise healthy lives, such as polluted indoor and outdoor air, contaminated water, and lack of adequate sanitation. This exposure to actual work that relates to their skills and interests can lay the foundation for career preparation and planning.

Service-learning groups may also offer students opportunities to fund raise, work within a budget, and plan and execute an advertising/promotional campaign. For some students, these types of skills may translate into an ideal career in the future.

TYING THE SERVICE TO CLASSWORK

In the same way that service learning exposes young adults to career skills and options, the experience also reinforces lessons learned in the classroom. Those studying chemistry may learn firsthand how mercury can be damaging to the environment and human body. Students pursuing classes in government and civics may learn through direct experience how laws are passed and regulations are established.

For middle school students at San Gabriel Christian School in San Gabriel, California, reducing waste in the school has become a regular part of the science curriculum. In 2010, students in science teacher Clarence Atwater's class participated in the first waste-reduction program by working in connection with Generation Earth, an environmental-education program of the Los Angeles County Department of Public Works. Throughout the year, students worked together to collect and recycle old cell phones and used ink cartridges. Students have gone on to expand their waste collection efforts to the community by holding drives to recycle electronics, including old computers, television sets, and other electronic waste.

For this campaign, they partnered with E-Waste Center, Inc., a company that helps to run events that collect broken and used electronics (called e-waste). As a result of this partnership, students sent 31,000 pounds of e-waste to be recycled (or e-cycled) instead of dumped in a landfill. A fringe benefit of e-waste collection is that these types of e-waste have value, and the company paid the school for the materials collected. Calling themselves the Young Environmental Specialists, or the YES team, the students were able to raise $2,000 for new computer equipment, a printer, and cameras to record their environmental efforts.

The YES team also visited a recycling facility called Planet Green to see in person how recycling can have a profound impact on the massive amounts of collected waste materials in our country.

The YES team has gone on to connect with bigger nationwide programs that support recycling. They joined efforts sponsored by Nike to salvage materials from used sneakers. Through this program, the

Some service-learning programs are able to get funding from corporate sponsors. Nike has a program to collect old sneakers and transform salvaged components into playground materials.

YES team collected old tennis shoes, which are then transformed into materials that become playground surfaces for low-income areas.

Through service learning, the course met class goals to educate students about sustainability and to empower them to reduce, reuse, and recycle in their school and community.

CHAPTER THREE

THE BIGGER PICTURE

Some environmental efforts undertaken by middle school and high school students happen on a very local level, such as establishing recycling in the cafeteria or planting trees on the school grounds. However, many programs reach out beyond the walls of schools and into the local community or state. Some programs are part of nationwide efforts, while others are tied into movements that stretch around the globe. Many opportunities show young adults how we are all connected on Mother Earth, and that like-minded protectors of the planet are all over the world.

One group that's stepped beyond the boundaries of their school to make a difference in their local environment is the Teen Shale Network. Under the guidance of their teachers, a group of State College High School students in Pennsylvania have formed the Teen Shale Network. These students are concerned with an energy industry process called fracking.

Fracking is a method of drilling down into the Earth and using a high-pressure water mixture that, when directed at the rock called shale, releases the gas inside. When water, sand, and chemicals are injected into the shale at high pressure, the gas flows out of the well. The process gets its name because it involves fracturing the shale to tap the gases. While fracking allows energy companies to reach hard-to-access fuel,

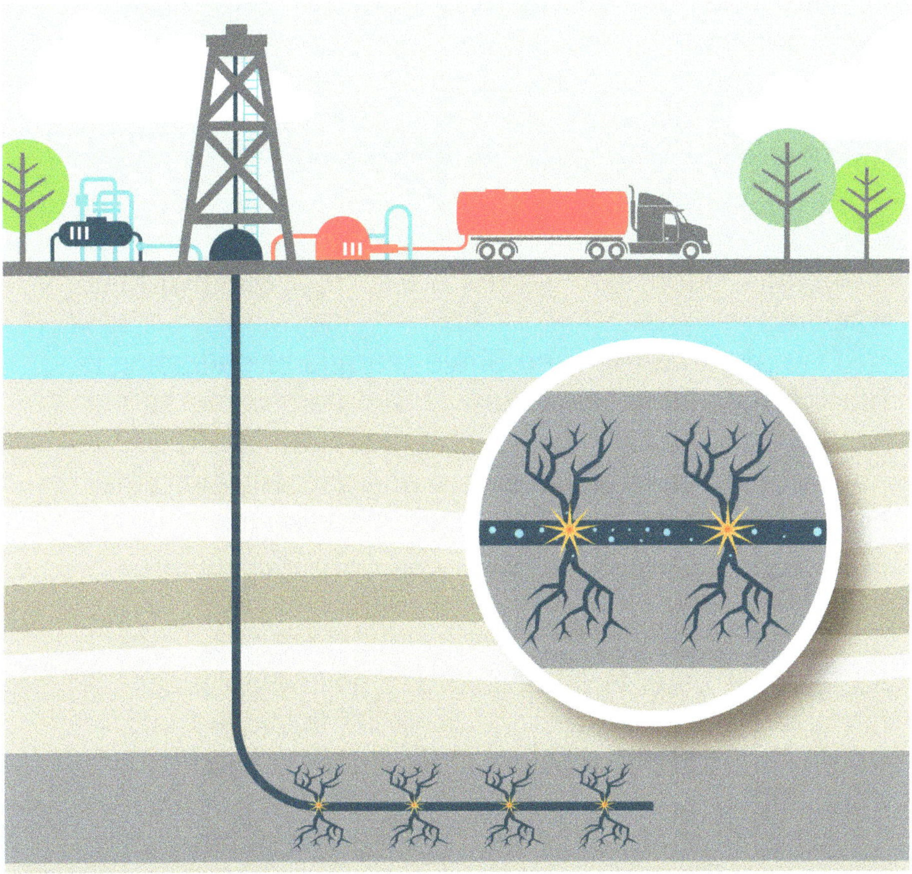

Students participating in the Teen Shale Network do research related to fracking, which is a process that taps gases in shale. It has been controversial because of the damage it may do to the environment.

this method of extracting energy is controversial for a few reasons. The method requires using huge amounts of water that must be transported to fracking sites, which some criticize as a waste of both energy and water. Also, carcinogenic (cancer-causing) materials are used and possibly released through the process. These may escape into the soil and groundwater. There are also concerns that this energy-tapping method may trigger earthquakes. Fracking is being used around the world, including in the northeastern United States.

The Teen Shale Network is sponsored by the Earth and Environmental Systems Institute (EESI) at Penn State University and other institutions. The goal of the EESI is to collect and organize data on water quality in regions where companies are using deep hydraulic fracking.

One site that the Teen Shale team is investigating is Black Moshannon State Park, 3,394 acres of forests and wetlands in nearby Philipsburg, Pennsylvania. Here, the students assist EESI scientists with gathering information from sensors that have been installed in the area and collecting water samples. The data they record includes temperature, pH (a measure of acidity), and dissolved oxygen and turbidity (cloudiness or haziness). If the pH of water is off because of pollutants, it can harm all living creatures and plant life that use that water. For example, if pH is off in waters where fish live, those fish may produce deformed young fish or die.

Samples gathered by the Teen Shale team are chemically analyzed for contaminants. Concepts that students have learned in organic chemistry are brought to life by the programs. Students may have learned about pH in the classroom, but a program such as this shows a real-life application, allowing students to see why the knowledge they have learned from their books is so important and can make a difference.

Students from other high schools in other states are participating in fracking research as well. The environmental science students at Mountain Ridge High School in Frostburg, Maryland, have contributed research from their area to the Shale Network. They have monitored water quality in areas that could be affected by gas drilling. Working under the guidance of their teacher, the students collected water-quality information before fracking started in the area. The plan is to use this data for comparison after fracking starts. The students put their information together in a presentation for the community called "Fracking: Pros, Cons, Uncertainty and Protecting the Safety of Frostburg's Drinking Water."

The information gathered by students from various locations will be added to the Shale Network database and will have the potential to help environmentalists who are addressing concerns about fracking around the world.

ONE GOOD IDEA CAN SPREAD AND GROW

Middle school, high school, and college students in Bozeman, Montana, have learned how an effective concept to help the environment can catch on and spread to different areas. A group called the Bozeman

Sometimes teens reach out to get the local community involved in their efforts. Young people in Bozeman, Montana, collected coffee grounds from coffee shops and used them to improve soil quality.

Youth Initiative realized that many coffee shops were wasting a valuable resource—coffee grounds. Each week, small coffee shops can generate as much as 30 gallons of used coffee grounds. Students in the Youth Initiative realized that coffee grounds are rich in nitrogen, which is good for plant growth. The nutrients in the coffee grounds can boost soil quality and compost piles. With special small trailers hooked to the backs of bicycles, students took to the streets and traveled from organic coffee shop to coffee shop to gather the spent grounds in a program they dubbed Coffee 2 Compost or C2C. The program has proven to be so popular that it has spread to several towns throughout Montana. Every year, the C2C program keeps about 5,000 pounds of used but useful coffee grounds from entering landfills. Seeing the success of their program, the coordinator of the Bozeman Youth Initiative created a handbook that gives a step-by-step approach for students in other communities who want to start their own C2C program.

A NATIONAL NONPROFIT MAY PROVIDE THE FOUNDATION

Some service-learning programs grow from long-established non-profit groups that have promoted the idea of community service for decades and have branches throughout the country. These groups include the Boy Scouts of America, the Girl Scouts

KEEP A JOURNAL

An important part of every service-learning experience is reflection on the experience, but it can be difficult to review all that has been accomplished in a program unless one keeps a journal. Journals are usually unstructured, but they offer a space to reflect on each day's experiences. Sometimes a student will have to force him or herself to write, but it is a process that gets easier with time and can help a student become a better writer. One tip is to write as if you are explaining your experience to another person so they can understand what you are accomplishing each day. A journal entry can detail an incident, a person, or a feeling. Here are some possible topics to address in the journal:

- What is the physical environment and mood of the workplace like?
- What is the organization's mission, and how is it going about fulfilling that mission?
- What are your responsibilities, and what do you accomplish each day?
- What parts of the work are most exciting, boring, fulfilling, and challenging?
- What are new things that you've learned?
- How might operations be improved?
- What are your impressions of other people—e.g., what do you like about them, what do you dislike about them, and what are you learning from them?
- What's the biggest surprise about the experience? Have there been any letdowns during the experience? What would you change about it?
- How does the experience relate to your academics?
- How does the experience relate to your career goals?

of the USA, Camp Fire, the Boys & Girls Clubs of America, and National 4-H. 4-H is the nation's largest youth-development organization, serving more than sixty-five million young people in urban, suburban, and rural communities nationwide. The students involved with the 4-H Club in Seward Township, Minnesota, made a major impact on the environment in their area by introducing a recycling

Justin Schultz *(left)*, a junior at Foothill High School in California, volunteers from a Boy Scout troop, and a youth group work together to install garden boxes at the Good News Rescue Mission.

program. With the nearest recycling plant about twenty-five miles away, residents in this area were accustomed to burning their trash. Ranging from ages seven to nineteen, the student members of the Seward Trailblazers 4-H Club were determined to change this. They set up a central collection point outside the town hall with containers where citizens could leave their plastic, paper, glass, corrugated cardboard, and aluminum cans. The students arranged with Nobles County Environmental Services (NCES) to pick up these materials on a regular schedule and bring them to the county recycling plant. For the program to work, however, the townspeople needed to know about it. Students created a campaign to educate the community. They sent out a mailing explaining the system, and they went door to door to share information about the program. Their labors paid off. Now, the recycling program collects about 340 pounds of materials every ten days.

Students think their program serves as a model of how to start a recycling program in a rural area, and other townships have been inspired by this 4-H effort and started their own similar programs based the Seward Township experience.

Non-profit nature-conservancy groups may also have opportunities for young people to volunteer their time to aid their efforts. The Audubon Society, for example, has a national bird-counting project and relies on data supplied by people in different regions across the nation to evaluate the health of native bird species. Interested students can form their own service-learning project to count bird species in their area.

National organizations may provide funding for service learning in your school. One group of note is Project Learning Tree, an organization with a mission to empower students to take action to improve their school and neighborhood environment based on what they learn in the classroom. The group's GreenWorks! program provides grants up to $3,000 to schools and youth organizations to engage students with their local community and complete service-learning, environmental-improvement projects.

McGraw-Hill, a global financial information and education company, has partnered with the National Wildlife Federation to create a textbook recycling project. The program focuses on helping individual students, schools, and organizations recycle hardcover books that are outdated or otherwise unsuitable for reuse. Through this program, students who want to develop a service-learning project can initiate a collection of old textbooks for recycling. The McGraw-Hill effort will de-ink textbook pages so their paper fiber can be reused to make new books. Through this program, students will gain an increased awareness of textbook recycling. Earth911, an environmental-services company, reports that paper made with recycled content can reduce total energy use by up to 44 percent and greenhouse gas emissions by 38 percent, in addition to eliminating virgin wood use.

Other companies advertise their dedication to preserving nature and may be approachable to support service-learning projects. For example, JetBlue Airways touts its One Thing That's Green program, which is focused on efforts to help communities and the environment by encouraging customers, crew members, and their communities to do "one thing that's green" for the environment. JetBlue says that it "works hand-in-hand with local and national organizations to foster influential programs and connect communities within our areas of commitment: Youth & Education, Community, and the Environment." Mitsubishi, Coca-Cola, and other corporations are also known for their support of educational programs. An Internet search can uncover other corporations and businesses that may support a school-wide program to help keep your campus or community green.

As mentioned earlier, Nike operates the Reuse-a-Shoe program. The company takes worn-out athletic shoes and grinds them down to create a new material called Nike Grind, which is used to make high-quality sports surfaces, including courts, turf fields, tracks, and more. These recycled shoes are reborn into sports and playground surfaces around the world. Students have formed shoe drives to collect old shoes and provide materials for this recycling program. Since the program began in 1990, more than twenty-five million pairs of shoes have been recycled. If your school, sports team, or community organization is interested in participating, they can apply to host a Reuse-A-Shoe drive in your community, and Reuse-a-Shoe will provide marketing materials.

CHAPTER FOUR

A CHANCE TO SEE AND CHANGE THE WORLD

While most service-learning opportunities take place within a student's school or community, there are many programs that send students to foreign countries to both study in the classroom and participate in hands-on efforts involving conservation. Most programs are for older students who are in high school. These students may play a role in maintaining rare plant and animal species, collecting data on wildlife, or conducting research for reforestation efforts.

Students who participate in programs abroad can enrich their lives by learning about other cultures and mastering other languages. These experiences can be a real résumé builder, as young people have an opportunity to show that they can surmount difficult challenges, thrive independently, and work together with others in a foreign environment.

One such program sends students to the wilds of Australia during the summer to learn about the country's conservation issues. Students get to learn

Some service-learning programs take students to foreign countries where they may help with conservation programs. By working abroad, students may learn another language and how to work with people from another culture.

firsthand about the various ecosystems—rain forests, coastlines, and coral reefs. Participants get to see native wildlife, such as koala bears and kangaroos, up close. Students interested in biology may especially benefit from the lessons taught in conservation management. Students also receive classroom instruction from local professors. While a program like this can cost up to $4,000 or more to attend for five weeks, those who enroll may be able to get scholarships and earn credit for a high school requirement or even college credit.

SPECIALIZED PROGRAMS IN OVERSEAS SERVICE LEARNING

Organizations such as Global Leadership Adventures (GLA) are specifically dedicated to summer volunteer programs abroad for high school students, many of which involve ecology and environmentalism. Teens can choose to travel to Bali, India, the Galapagos Islands, Costa Rica, or the Dominican Republic to make a lasting difference on a local community's environmental and ecological sustainability. In the Dominican Republic, teen volunteers have worked to build water systems and to reforest lowland areas. In the Galapagos Islands, young people have contributed their efforts to the restoration of natural habitats for endangered species, such as the giant tortoise and the waved albatross, so they can reproduce and thrive.

Students who volunteer abroad may have the opportunity to help save endangered species, such as the giant tortoise or green sea turtle. Here, volunteers help rescue a marine turtle at Kuta Beach in Indonesia.

GLA works in collaboration with tortoise breeding centers. The wildlife in the Galapagos Islands constantly faces environmental threats. Students can help by removing invasive plants, litter, and foreign plant species. Although students put in hours of labor, they also have a chance to enjoy the surrounding nature. They can swim with sea lions and observe blue-footed boobies perched on rocks. They can also explore volcanoes, beaches, lagoons, and forests.

In Costa Rica, students work together to help preserve the biodiversity of the rainforest. In the mornings, students construct tree nurseries and plant trees to reforest the region. They also clear trails through the forest to prevent hikers and other visitors from going off trail and interfering with the habitat. Some afternoons are spent with biologists collecting species for a large, ongoing research project in the national park. Student volunteers may also collaborate with local students on environmental projects. In the cloud forest, teens learn of problems related to water, public health, and ecological conservation. Plus, students are surrounded by tropical birds and exotic monkeys that fill the jungle treetops with activity.

One student on the GLA website wrote that the program "opened my mind to many different facets of environmentalism, and now I'm going to major in environmental science in college next year."

Another student described her experience in this way: "For the first week, we were located at a nature reserve in Guanacaste planting trees at our location and also surrounding a local school. The second week we travelled up to the cloud forest in Guanacaste and focused mainly on building a recycling system for one of their schools and also taught the students a lot of Basic English. I was really touched by the enthusiasm and energy the children showed, and the bonds I created with them are memories I will remember forever. I learned so much about leadership and how a small contribution made can mean so much more to others."

Projects Abroad is another major organization that provides environmentally oriented service-learning experiences for teens, ages sixteen to nineteen, in locations throughout Africa, Asia, Eastern Europe, Latin America, and the South Pacific. Students in this program have gone to Cambodia and learned to dive in an effort to study and protect the Gulf of Thailand reef and the endangered seahorses that live in these seas. In Costa Rica, students have contributed to projects in the caves and forest of the Barra Honda National Park. In Fiji, they have worked side by side with scientists who are experts in shark conservation. In India, they have learned the importance of growing trees and medicinal plants. In Kenya, they have assisted in protecting the endangered African wildlife in the Rift Valley. Those who have headed to Mexico have contributed to projects involving endangered species of crocodile. Some have headed high into the Himalayas of Nepal to assist with efforts on the unique but fragile environment. In the Amazon, teens have collected data on the rainforest, surrounded by macaws, monkeys, and beautiful butterflies. In South Africa, students have lived and worked on game reserves and contributed to ongoing missions to maintain the populations of elephants, hyenas, and other species of animals.

Each volunteer project keeps to a schedule of taught sessions in a classroom environment, and hands-on and observational service work, as well as evening activities and weekend excursions. Lasting two to four weeks, these teen volunteer abroad programs are designed to contribute to the student's community service credits in his or her high school. These programs also provide a unique learning experience to include on a college application.

Programs like these offer students a safe and supervised environment to roll up their sleeves and complete work that will really make a difference in improving the world.

Ecological volunteer programs are playing a role in getting people involved and contributing to the health of the planet as a whole. These efforts contribute to

TEN TIPS FOR VOLUNTEERING ABROAD

STA Travel, a student travel association, offers these ten tips for young people willing to donate their time, energy, and experience in other countries:

- Plan ahead, and think about why you want to volunteer, what you want to achieve, and how long you [are willing to] be gone.
- Exhibit enthusiasm and willingness.
- Arm yourself with a positive attitude—your experience will, as a result, be an enriching and fulfilling one.
- Have patience and determination—what you offer is recognized, appreciated, and needed.
- Be open-minded—the more you put into the project, the more you will get out of it.
- Ask what has been achieved by other volunteers and how much of the fee goes to the project(s).
- Be sensitive to the culture [that] you are visiting, and be aware of ecosystem fragility.
- Be committed, and follow the rules of the project.
- Try to ensure that your stay brings benefits to the wider community.

biodiversity, conserving native plants and animals, and reducing the odds of their extinction. A healthy environment can help reduce the effects of climate change and counteract harmful gas emissions. Students who travel abroad to volunteer their services also help to improve the quality of life for the people who live in those regions.

DISCOVERING A DIFFERENT CULTURE

Adam Willis, a student from Berlin, Massachusetts, volunteered his time to projects in China, Africa, and Peru. On the blog "The Young Leader," Willis wrote, "One of the most amazing things about traveling and experiencing new cultures is the opportunity to have dialogue with those who are different than you. That level of diversity is a driving force in my passion for immersion in developing countries. I've learned so much about myself and opened up to the world around me. Every time I travel, I learn more about different people and places in the world—and it's impossible to pick a favorite."

Students who get involved in service learning abroad get a sense of how we are all connected in the world. They see how they really can make a difference in the world and in people's lives. They also learn about the customs, rituals, and foods of other cultures. They have a chance to interact with people who are foreign to them on a daily basis. Projects Abroad

Young people who work in foreign countries often stay with host families, which gives them a chance to form lasting relationships and see how people live and work on a daily basis.

participants, for example, stay with host families, so they are able to see how people live and work on a day-to-day basis. Those interested in foreign languages will have a chance to immerse themselves in an

SETTING OFF TO NEW FRONTIERS: VOLUNTEERING ABROAD PROGRAMS

Here are a few of the top programs that offer service-learning opportunities related to helping the environment in a foreign country.

Amigos de las Américas (AMIGOS)
http://www.amigoslink.org
AMIGOS operates in nine countries throughout the Americas—in Mexico, the Dominican Republic, Nicaragua, Costa Rica, Panama, Colombia, Ecuador, Peru, and Paraguay. The programs, which are open to students ages sixteen to twenty-five with a basic knowledge of Spanish, include environmental sustainability.

United Planet
http://www.unitedplanet.org
This organization provides service-learning options, including environmental conservation projects, in destinations such as Romania, Costa Rica, Peru, Ecuador, and Chile.

Center for Cultural Interchange
http://www.cci-exchange.com
This program places volunteers ages sixteen and older in a project to rescue wildlife in the heart of the Costa Rican rainforest.

(continued on the next page)

(continued from the previous page)

Earthwatch Institute
http://www.earthwatch.org
In volunteer expeditions sponsored by the Earthwatch Institute, teens assist scientists in missions to improve the planet in various locations in the world.

Students Partnership Worldwide
http://www.restlessdevelopment.org
This operation recruits and trains young adults as volunteer "Peer Educators." Participants lead programs that impact health and environmental issues in Africa and Asia. Students have to be a bit older (at least eighteen years old), but it's a program to keep on the radar for the future.

atmosphere where a foreign language must be spoken every day. It's one of the best ways to master a language.

During his service in Peru, Adam worked on a project to build clean-burning stoves for indigenous families. The stoves were not only better for the environment and air quality—they also improved the respiratory health of women and children, who are often home preparing meals and tending to the stove. Those involved in community service in Peru also constructed greenhouses so families living in the countryside could plant vegetable gardens to combat malnutrition in children and raise traditional medicinal plants as well.

Some students forge bonds with local people that can last a lifetime, and they continue to make return

In a service-learning program in Peru, students helped construct greenhouses similar to this one at a high school in the Andes Mountains. The greenhouses helped families in the countryside grow vegetables to combat malnutrition.

trips to these foreign countries and newfound friends throughout their lives. They also make friends with other volunteer students who often come from countries around the world. These shared experiences can lead to long-lasting personal relationships, and some students have gone on to visit the other volunteers in their home countries.

CHAPTER FIVE

STARTING YOUR OWN PROGRAM

Not every school will have the perfect environmental program to suit each student, but students can design their own projects. First, they need to look around their school or the community for a need. Think of programs that might be needed. The school may already have a recycling program for natural waste and everyday recyclable materials, like bottles, cans, and newspapers. The school may not, however, have any projects that offer an opportunity to recycle old electronics.

Ambitious students who want to help the world to conserve energy may consider building a wind-energy or solar-energy facility that the school community could benefit from. Students at Essex County College in New Jersey, for example, built a solar-powered station designed for college and area high school students to charge their cell phones, laptops, and other electronic devices. These stations, which sit in a convenient spot outside on a campus, can easily be adapted to a high school campus as well. A project like this is not only good for the environment—it also

One way to help the environment is by creating energy sources that are solar or wind powered. By building solar and wind-based projects, students learn about the science and engineering involved in this cutting-edge technology.

incorporates lessons on science and engineering. Plus, students who helped build the solar recharging station have now gained experience in the cutting-edge field of solar technology.

Students in the Environmental Club at Deering High School in Portland, Maine, constructed six solar panels that were installed on the roof of a concession stand at the school's Memorial Stadium. The senior student who led the project, Josh Snyder, came up with the idea after learning about renewable energy at an environmental-learning program called the Green Energy Project, which he attended for two weeks in the summer. Through this program, Snyder learned how solar panels could help to solve the global energy crisis. Snyder and other members of the Deering Environmental Club raised $1,000 to purchase the materials. The panels now provide some of the electricity for the sports stadium's concession stand.

"These solar panels will act as a symbol of Deering's willingness to adapt to a changing world—a world in which fossil fuels are no longer acceptable," said Snyder in a press release.

While the Deering project was not labeled a service-learning experience, it certainly could be considered one because students came together to help the environment and benefit the student body as a whole. The solar project also shows how a single student can dream up a project and bring it to life with the help of school administrators and fellow students.

STEPS TO STARTING A SERVICE-LEARNING PROGRAM

Once a student has developed a concept for a service-learning program, there are three crucial elements to making it become a reality: gaining approval from the school; finding a team of like-minded, smart, and enthusiastic students to collaborate with; and recruiting a school teacher or other school staff member who can serve as the adult supervisor/ coordinator and has the time to spend on the project. Make sure a potential supervisor/coordinator has the time to volunteer and some background related to the nature of the project. The project monitor should be just as enthusiastic about an environmental-service experience as the students are.

To start your own service-learning program, you usually need a teacher or other adult supervisor to help oversee the program. Here, an adult coordinator assists students in setting up an urban organic community garden.

With students and a supervisor on board, check with the school administrators about how to get approval. Administrators may ask that a proposal be put in writing and specify the program leader, members, purpose, costs, and goals. Details, such as where and when the program will be held, have to be spelled out.

The proposal will also have to explain what participants can expect to learn and how the lessons learned apply to the curriculum, whether it be English, science, health, math, or another area. The program description will need to establish goals and clearly demonstrate the benefits it will offer to the school and/or the community.

A description of the program will also have to appeal to other students so the program can attract participants. Once a proposal and outline for the program has been agreed upon, the students, teachers, and administrators involved may want to sign a letter of confirmation.

Think about how the programs will be funded. Does the group need to hold a fundraising event, such as a bake sale or car wash, to support the program? Is it possible to get financial support from local businesses and organizations?

Also ask: will the program benefit from working with an organization outside the school? For example, there may be a business in the area that specializes in e-cycling that can help with efforts to recycle electronics.

When setting up a service-learning program, be detailed about its members, purpose, cost, and goals. A clothes drive, for example, can be a creative way to keep old garments from ending up in the trash.

Always think creatively. Collecting old clothing for reuse can be a program that helps the environment, because when people buy and wear thrift clothes, they

FRINGE BENEFIT: RÉSUMÉ BUILDING

The main reasons to participate in any service-learning experience are to benefit the community and the world, while learning lessons in the process. These unique experiences, however, also provide strong material for résumés and college application essays. Young people often don't have an employment history that they can draw upon for their résumé. Through volunteering, students can build elements that are crucial to a résumé, such as skills learned, duties, responsibilities, objectives achieved, leadership roles, etc.

The experiences gained through service learning can be so unique and enriching that they can also make good content for college essays. Because self-reflection is usually a component of service learning, students have considered the lessons they've learned, how their work has helped the environment, and how the experience may have inspired their direction for the future in terms of academic pursuits and career options.

Environmental projects also offer the opportunity to build friendships and contacts that may help open doors later in life as students search for job opportunities. The program supervisors and mentors may wind up being supporters who are willing to write recommendations and serve as references for a résumé.

are not using products that may have been simply thrown away, and they're not buying new clothes that require new energies to make and deliver. Students could hold a thrift clothes fashion show to demonstrate how stylish used clothing can be. It could also be a way to raise money.

Students who start their own service-learning program should carefully record accomplishments and take note of challenges and how those challenges were overcome.

EXPLORING THE OPTIONS

What service-learning project do you want to start at your school? Not sure? Search the web for different ideas and options. One source worth exploring is the National Service-Learning Clearinghouse (http://gsn.nylc.org/clearinghouse). The site contains tons of helpful information and ideas for service-learning programs. An EarthEcho Expeditions webinar, for example, shows how to take steps to improve water on our planet. Another webinar introduces viewers to the work done by Project Learning Tree and how youth are making a change in the environment with service learning.

There are many documents on this website that show how educators plan service-learning programs, and these can help students understand the process as well. Members of the Southeast Wisconsin Service Learning Consortium (SWSLC) present information about how they partnered with Urban Ecology Center, Keep Greater Milwaukee Beautiful, the

Look into the various organizations in your area that may already be established to help the environment. Existing groups already have the structure and experience to take action and get things done.

Bicycle Federation of Milwaukee, Inland Seas Charter High School, and Waterford Waterways Management District.

So before launching a program at your school, do your homework, take inspiration from others who have done it before, and see what lessons can be learned from their successes and challenges.

GLOSSARY

biodegradable Describing materials that break down and return to the ecosystem without polluting it.

biodiversity The variety of plants, animals, and living things in an area. Maintaining biodiversity helps preserve the web of life.

carcinogenic Tending to cause cancer.

climate change A change in the global atmosphere, especially after the mid- to late-20th century, because of increased air pollution, specifically carbon dioxide from fossil fuels.

compost Decayed organic material (plants, coffee grounds, dead leaves, manure, etc.) used as fertilizer.

ecofriendly Describing actions or products that do not harm the environment.

ecology A branch of biology concerning the relationship of organisms to one another and to their environment.

ecosystem A community or network of organisms and their environment that interact as an ecological unit.

e-cycle To recycle, reuse, or redistribute electronics and electrical components that have reached the end of their life cycle.

endangered species A type of animal or plant that is so low in number that it is at risk of extinction.

energy audit An analysis of energy needs, consumption, and efficiency of a building or buildings.

fossil fuels Natural fuels, such as oil, gas, and coal, formed in the Earth from the remains of plants and animals from a previous geological time.

fracking A shortened term for hydraulic fracturing, a process using high-pressure chemicals and liquids to fracture rocks below the Earth's surface to extract natural gas and oil.

green space A community space of trees, grass, gardens, and other vegetation in an otherwise urban environment. Green spaces enhance the beauty and environmental qualities of neighborhoods.

invasive plants A plant species that spreads aggressively outside of its natural range and takes over an area, often forcing out native plants and animals.

landfill A low-lying area where solid-waste materials are buried in layers of soil. Landfills are considered environmentally safe.

organic Describing products that are strictly made from plant and animal products without hormones, drugs, or synthetic chemicals.

peer educator A student who takes on the role of teacher to educate other students.

pH In environmental terms, pH is usually an expression of hydrogen ion concentration in water. It is used to measure acidity.

reforest To replant tree seeds or young trees in an area of forest that has been cleared from cutting or fire.

renewable energy Energy from a source that doesn't run out, such as wind and solar power.

sustainability A condition in which the coexistence of humans and nature in productive harmony is created and maintained so that water, materials, and resources will continue to protect human health and the environment.

turbidity Cloudiness or haziness of a fluid caused by particles. It is often a measure of water quality.

FOR MORE INFORMATION

Action Without Borders/Idealist.org
302 Fifth Avenue, 11th Floor
New York, NY 10001
(646) 786-6886
Website: http://www.idealist.org
Since 1995, this organization has been dedicated to finding practical solutions to social and environmental problems by connecting people, organizations, and resources.

Canada World Youth
2330 Notre-Dame Street West, Suite 300
Montreal, QC H3J 1N4
Canada
(800) 605-3526
Website: http://www.canadaworldyouth.org
Since 1971, this organization has offered international volunteer programs to thousands of youths who want to participate in community-driven development projects that nurture leadership skills and allow them to become agents of change.

Corporation for National Community Service (CNCS)
1201 New York Avenue NW
Washington, DC 20525
(202) 606-5000
Website: http://www.nationalservice.gov
Through its core programs, such as AmeriCorps and the Social Innovation Fund, and its leading role in President Obama's national call to service

initiative, United We Serve, this federal agency has promoted civic engagement and enlisted more than five million Americans in service and volunteering opportunities.

DoSomething.org
19 West 21st Street, 8th Floor
New York, NY 10010
(212) 254-2390
Website: http://www.dosomething.org
Over two and a half million young people use this site to get involved with volunteer projects, ranging from poverty to violence to the environment.

Service for Youth
140 Promenade du Portage, Phase IV, 4D392
Mail Drop 403
Gatineau, QC K1A 0J9
Canada
Attn: Youth Operations Directorate
Canada
(800) 935-5555
Website: http://www.youth.gc.ca
This government of Canada site prepares youth for work but also offers advice and connections to volunteering opportunities, including Volunteer Canada.

VolunteerMatch
550 Montgomery Street, 8th Floor
San Francisco, CA 94111

(415) 241-6868
Website: http://www.volunteermatch.org
This organization lists more than ninety thousand non-profit organizations around the world that have volunteer opportunities and helps potential volunteers find options that match their interests.

WEBSITES

Because of the changing nature of Internet links, Rosen Publishing has developed an online list of websites related to the subject of this book. This site is updated regularly. Please use this link to access the list:

http://www.rosenlinks.com/SLFT/Envi

FOR FURTHER READING

Amsel, Sheri. *The Everything Kids' Environment Book: Learn How You Can Help the Environment By Getting Involved at School, at Home, or at Play*. Avon, MA: Adams Media, 2007.

Boles, Nichole Bouchard. *How to Be an Everyday Philanthropist: 330 Ways to Make a Difference in Your Home, Community, and World—At No Cost.* New York, NY: Workman Publishing Company, 2009.

Donovan, Sandy. *Volunteering Smarts: How to Find Opportunities, Create a Positive Experience, and More* (USA Today Teen Wise Guides: Lifestyle Choices). Nashville, TN: 21st Century, 2012.

Earthworks Group, and Sophie Javna. *The New 50 Simple Things Kids Can Do to Save the Earth.* Riverside, NJ: Andrews McMeel Publishing, 2009.

Friedman, Jenny, and Jolene Roehlkepartain. *Doing Good Together: 101 Easy, Meaningful Service Projects for Families, Schools, and Communities.* Minneapolis, MN: Free Spirit Publishing, 2010.

Gay, Kathlyn. *Volunteering: The Ultimate Teen Guide* (It Happened to Me). Lanham, MD: Scarecrow Press, 2007.

Gralla, Preston. *The Complete Idiot's Guide to Volunteering for Teens.* New York, NY: Alpha, 2001.

Jones, Karen. *The Difference a Day Makes: 365 Ways to Change Your World in Just 24 Hours.* Novato, CA: New World Library, 2004.

Kaye, Catherine Berger, Philippe Cousteau, and EarthEcho International. *Going Blue: A Teen Guide to Saving Our Oceans, Lakes, Rivers, & Wetlands.* Minneapolis, MN: Free Spirit Publishing, 2009.

Lewis, Barbara. *The Kid's Guide to Service Projects: Over 500 Service Ideas for Young People Who Want to Make a Difference.* Minneapolis, MN: Free Spirit Publishing, 2009.

Lewis, Barbara. *The Teen Guide to Global Action: How to Connect with Others (Near & Far) to Create Social Change.* Minneapolis, MN: Free Spirit Publishing, 2007.

Perry, Susan. *Catch the Spirit: Teen Volunteers Tell How They Made a Difference.* New York, NY: Grolier Publishing, 2000.

Rohmer, Harriet. *Heroes of the Environment: True Stories of People Who Are Helping to Protect Our Planet.* San Francisco, CA: Chronicle Books, 2009.

Savedge, Jenn. *The Green Teen: The Eco-Friendly Teen's Guide to Saving the Planet.* Gabriola Island, BC, Canada: New Society Publishers, 2009.

Sivertsen, Linda, and Tosh Sivertsen. *Generation Green: The Ultimate Teen Guide to Living an Eco-Friendly Life.* New York, NY: Simon Pulse, 2008.

Sundem, Garth. *Real Kids, Real Stories, Real Change: Courageous Actions Around the World.* Minneapolis, MN: Free Spirit Publishing, 2010.

Wandberg, Robert. *Volunteering, Giving Back.* North Mankato, MN: Capstone Press, Inc., 2001.

We Are What We Do. *31 Ways to Change the World.* Somerville, MA: Candlewick, 2010.

We Are What We Do. *Change the World for Ten Bucks.* San Francisco, CA: Chronicle Books, 2009.

Weyn, Suzanne. *Empty.* New York, NY: Scholastic, 2012.

BIBLIOGRAPHY

Chicago Public Schools. "Service Learning." Retrieved May 4, 2014 (http://servicelearning.cps.k12.il.us/Student.html).

Connecticut Audubon Society. "What's New." Retrieved May 4, 2014 (http://www.ctaudubon.org).

Danahy, Anne. "State High students Learn About Fracking, Water Quality in the Field." Penn State News, February 21, 2014. Retrieved May 4, 2014 (http://news.psu.edu/story/305136/2014/02/21/campus-life/state-high-students-learn-about-fracking-water-quality-field).

Earth Corps. "Alumni Updates." Retrieved May 4, 2014 (http://www.earthcorps.org/alumni.php).

Experiential Learning Center, University of Colorado Denver. "What Is Service Learning?" Retrieved May 4, 2014 (http://www.ucdenver.edu/life/services/ExperientialLearning/forfaculty/servicelearning/Pages/servicelearning.aspx).

Fairfax County Public Schools. "Service Learning: High School." Retrieved May 4, 2014 (http://www.fcps.edu/is/servicelearning/hs.shtml).

Generator School Network. Retrieved May 4, 2014 (http://gsn.nylc.org).

Greenbery, Mark. "National Wildlife Federation, McGraw-Hill and NewPage Corporation Launch Textbook Recycling Project." National Wildlife Federation. March 28, 2011. Retrieved May 4, 2014 (http://www.nwf.org/news-and-magazines/media-center/news-by-topic/global-warming/2011/03-28-11-nwf-mcgraw-hill-and-newpage-corporation-launch-textbook-recycling-project.aspx).

Hatala, Greg. "Students Build Solar Power Charging Station." *Star Ledger*, September 30, 2013. Retrieved May 4, 2014 (http://www.nj.com/essex/index.ssf/2013/09/students_build_solar_power_charging_station.html).

Maryland State Department of Education. "Programs: Environment." Retrieved May 4, 2014 (http://www.marylandpublicschools.org/MSDE/programs/servicelearning/environment.html).

Miller, Kelly. "Olympia High School Earth Corps Making A Difference." ThurstonTalk.com., March 10, 2013. Retrieved May 4, 2014 (http://www.thurstontalk.com/2013/03/10/olympia-high-school-clubs).

National Wildlife Federation. "About Eco Schools USA." Retrieved May 4, 2014 (http://www.nwf.org/Eco-Schools-USA/About-Eco-Schools-USA.aspx).

Nike. "Reuse-a-Shoe." May 29, 2013. Retrieved May 4, 2014 (http://www.nike.com/us/en_us/c/better-world/stories/2013/05/reuse-a-shoe).

Pandika, Melissa. "Green Careers: Environmental Law." Sierra Club. March 22, 2013. Retrieved May 4, 2014 (http://sierraclub.typepad.com/greenlife/2013/03/green-careers-environmental-law.html).

Portland Public Schools. "Deering Students Build Solar Panels for Memorial Stadium." May 18, 2010. Retrieved May 4. 2014 (http://www2.portlandschools.org/news/deering-students-build-solar-panels-memorial-stadium).

Project Learning Tree. "Service-Learning." Retrieved May 4, 2014 (https://www.plt.org/greenworks-service-learning).

Stephen T. Badin High School. "Service Learning." Retrieved May 4, 2014 (http://www.badinhs.org/campus_min/campusmin_service_learning.asp).

TransitionsAbroad.com. "Teen Volunteer Organizations." Retrieved May 4, 2014 (http://www.transitionsabroad.com/listings/study/teen/teen_volunteer_organizations.shtml).

West, Larry. "Why Recycle Cell Phones?" About.com. Retrieved May 4, 2014 (http://environment.about.com/od/mobilephones/a/why_recycle_cell_phones.htm).

World Health Organization. "Environmental Health Issues." Retrieved May 4, 2014 (http://www.who.int/features/2005/health_survey/environmental_health/en).

INDEX